THIS IS THE HAT.

A STORY IN RHYME

by • Nancy Van Laan

Pictures by • Holly Meade

Little, Brown and Company
Boston • Toronto • London

First Edition

Library of Congress Cataloging-in-Publication Data
Van Laan, Nancy.
This is the hat / by Nancy Van Laan ; pictures by Holly Meade. — 1st ed.
p.   cm.
Summary: Cumulative verses follow an old man's hat as it becomes a home for a spider, mouse, and other creatures before returning to its rightful owner.
ISBN 0-316-89727-2
[1. Hats — Fiction. 2. Animals — Fiction. 3. Stories in rhyme.] I. Meade, Holly, ill. II. Title.
PZ8.3.V47Th   1992
[E] — dc20   91-35833

10 9 8 7 6 5 4 3 2 1   WOR

Joy Street Books are published by Little, Brown and Company (Inc.)

Published simultaneously in Canada by Little, Brown & Company (Canada) Limited

Printed in Hong Kong

For the hat lovers in my life —
son David, brother Philip,
and friends Jane and Tom.

N. V. L.

For my young
helpers in making
these pictures,
Noah and Jenny.

H. M.

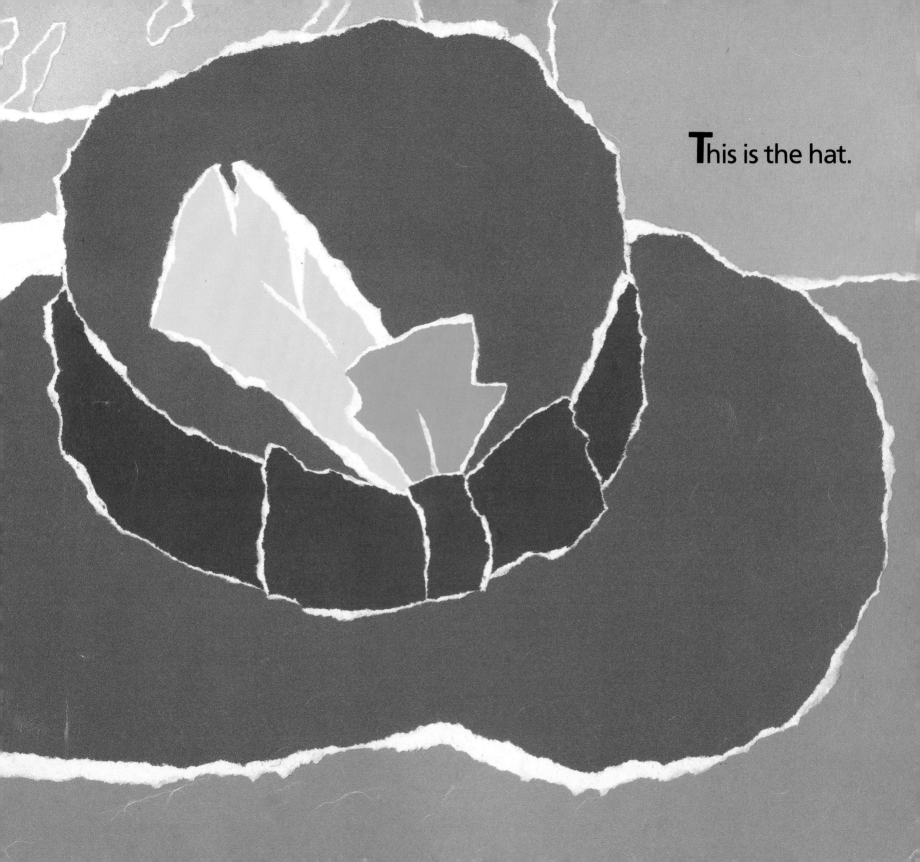

This is the hat.

This is the man who wore the hat.

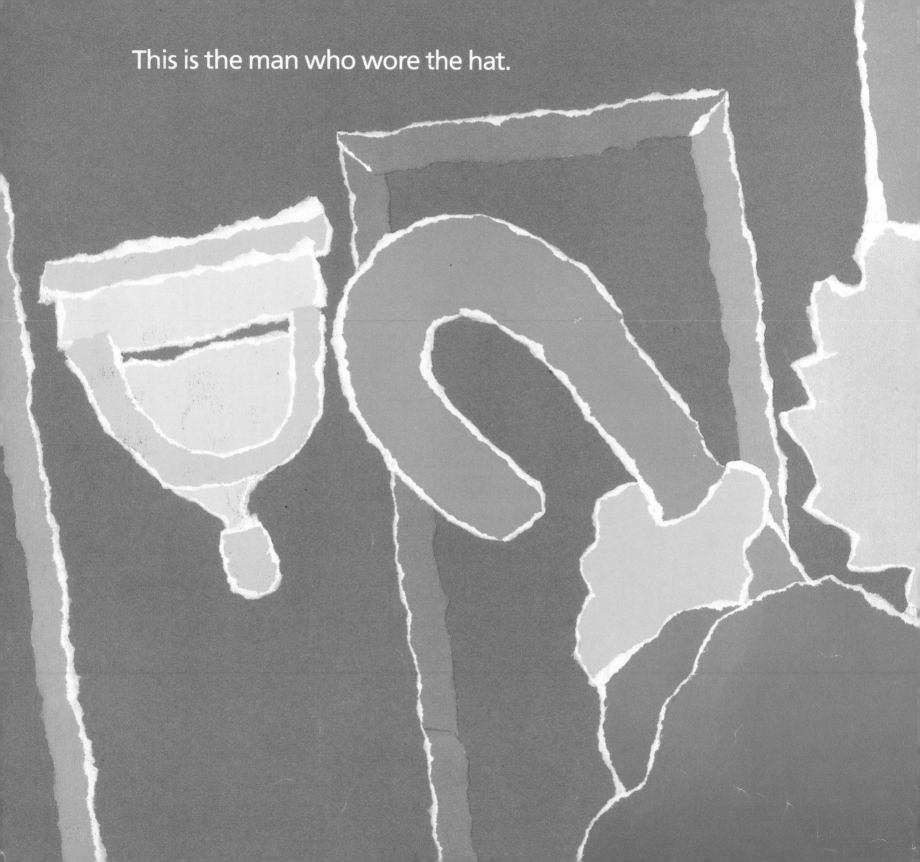

He wore the hat when he walked in the rain,

TAP-A-TAP-TAP!

with his old wooden cane.

Around whisked the wind and snatched the hat.

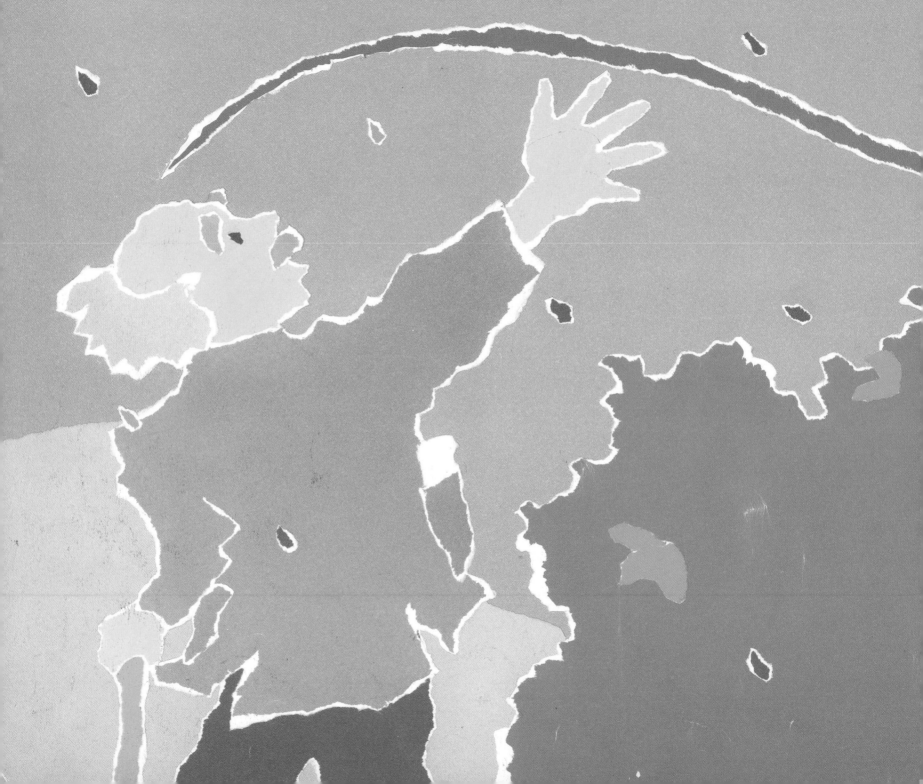

WHOOOOOSHI

The hat flew away
to a field of hay
where, upside down,
it sat.

A woolly brown spider crawled into the hat.

SPIN-A-SPIN-SPIN!

The spider moved in.

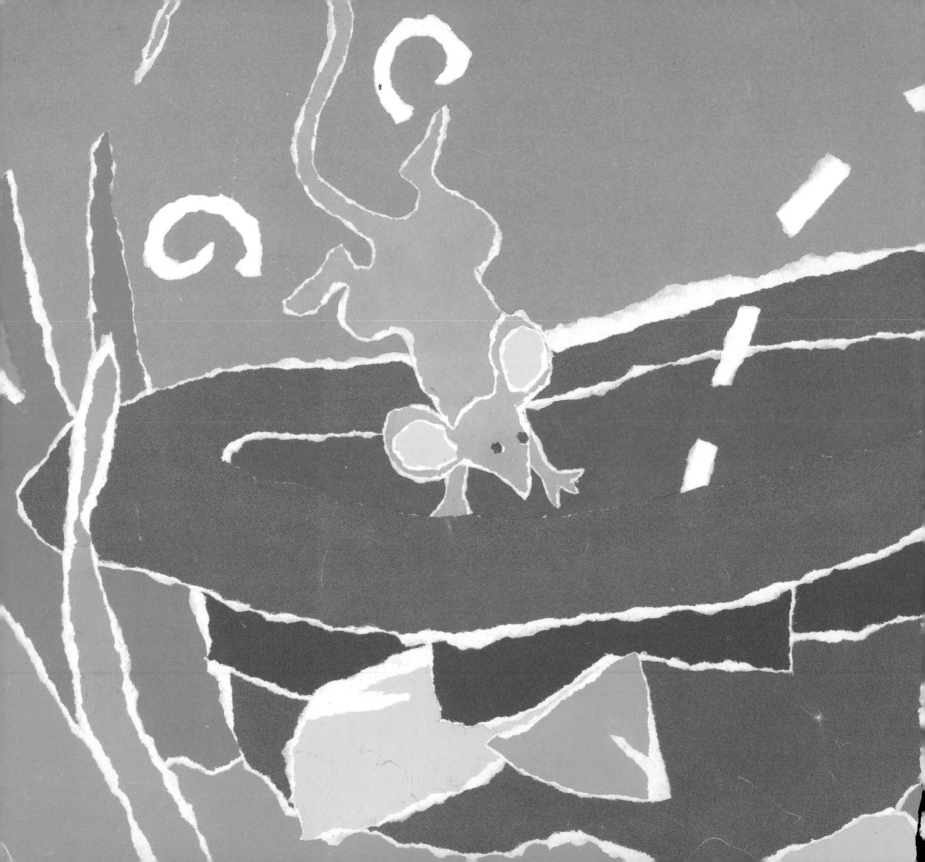

Liggedy-lippity leapt a mouse.
It bounced the spider out of its house.
"SCREEK-A-TWEEK-TWEEK!"

the little mouse said,
"this hat will make a mighty fine bed!"

Then along came a farmer. He picked up the hat.
Out jumped the mouse . . . *pittery-pat!*
The farmer laughed,

"HO·HO·HO·HO!

This hat will make a swell scarecrow!"

Down fluttered crow. He perched on the hat.
The *scarecrow's* hat. Imagine that!
"*Caw! Caw! Caw!* A dandy nest!
I'll add some straw, but first I'll rest."

ZZZZZZ...ZZZZZZ...Z

"*Tut! Tut!*" clucked the farmer's wife when she saw
the crow in the hat with a nest out of straw.

"SHOO! SHOO!

Fly away!" the farmer's wife said.
Then off she skipped with the hat on *her* head.

She watched a hen strut by on thin legs,
while she used the hat to gather some eggs.
She filled the hat with kernels of corn
and fed the chicks, who sang out their song,

"CHEEP-CHEEP-CHEEP!"

on that chilly morn.

Later that day, with the hat on her knees,
she sat on the porch and shelled spring peas.

TUMBLY·TUM·TUM!

flopped the pup in her lap.
He spilled the peas and snatched up the hat.

He carried the hat way down the road,
but it dropped
when he stopped
to bark at a toad.

Yip! Yip! He growled, *"GRRRR-OW!"*
When the toad hopped away, the puppy howled.

AHHHH·

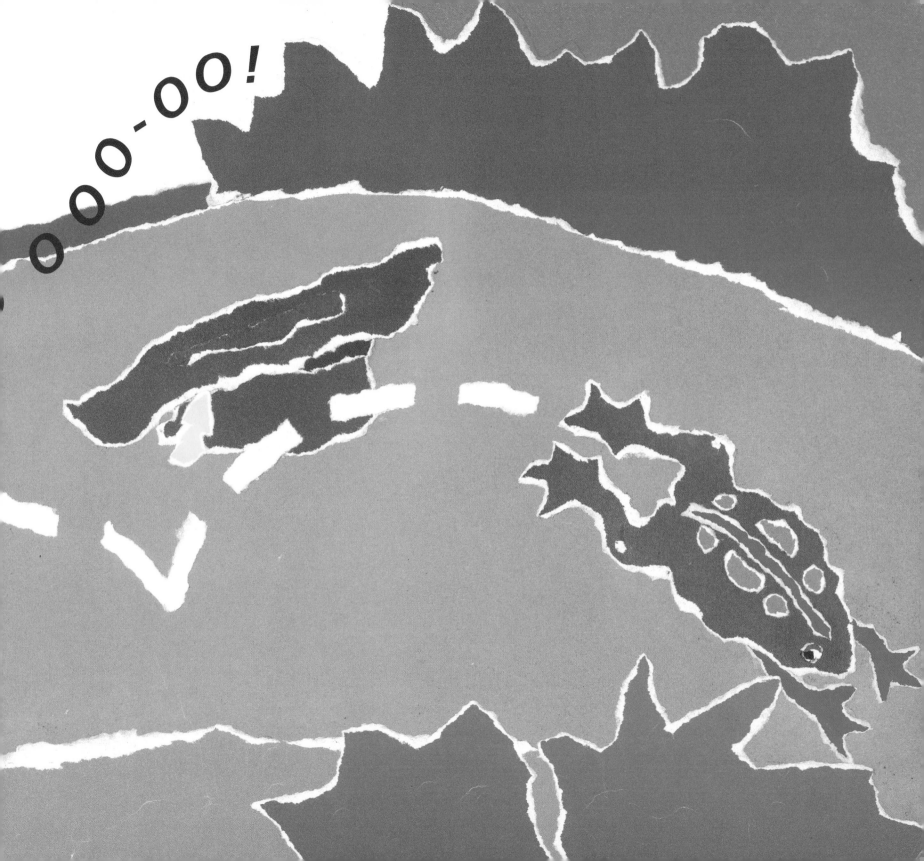

SPLITTERY- SPLAT!
SPLITTERY- SPLAT!

The pup ran home when it started to rain.

Then along came the man
with the old wooden cane.

TAPPY-TAP-TAP!

He found his hat!
It was dusty and dirty
and rumpled and stained . . .

But he whooped a glad song,
picked it up, put it on,

then danced

JIG-A-JIG-JIG

in the rain.

He danced

JIG-A-JIG, TAP-A-TAP,

JIGGY-JIG, TAPPY-TAP,

JIG-A-TAP-TAP

down the lane!